Stories From Around the Fountain

Produced with funding and support from the Victoria Park
Project

Contents

Introduction

Stories from Around the Fountain is a collaboration between friends who share a love of writing. Of course, at the beginning of the project, we were strangers, such is the magic and warmth of the written word that it can unite people from different ages, backgrounds and cultures.

One sunny Sunday morning, thanks to the hospitality of the Victoria Park Project, the 7 of us met and tentatively started putting pen to paper. We dreamed, laughed and at times fought to get through the writing prompts but gradually little stories emerged from the chaos. We took inspiration from the beautiful setting of the park, using nature to guide our way, and journeyed through the archives to rediscover the history of our beautiful town.

For Ashford is beautiful. Its history and pockets of natural charm are what have sustained us over the 8 weeks it took to compose this pamphlet. It remains a place where strangers can come together and become friends – where new histories can be written and remembered. A place where stories can grow and thrive from the smallest seeds.

Sita Turner – founder of *Park Write*

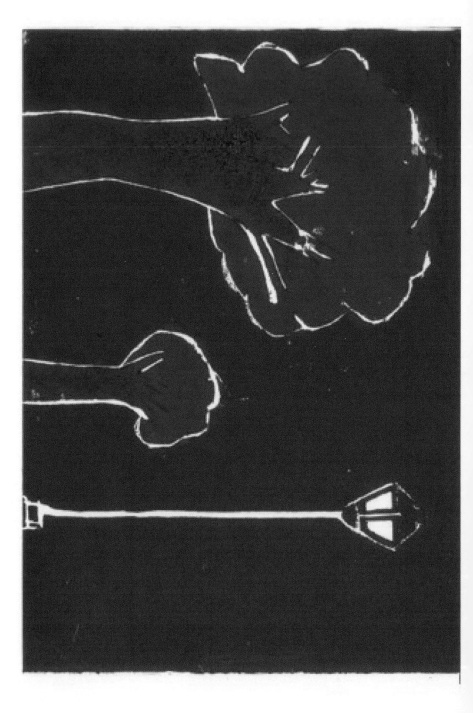

The Heart Remains the Same

Janine Gardiner

They stand around the perimeter of the park, overlooking centuries of change. It's the 21st century, but they've been here one hundred years or more. Between them, silent and statuesque, stands an ancient cast iron streetlamp, its metal casing oxidised and cracked from an age of being beaten by the weather. A clear testament to how much change they have seen in this park.

Slowly, the elder of the two trees stretches his branches, awakening from a nap. Now he's older, he needs more time to rest, recuperate and rejuvenate; unlike in his youth, when he could watch over this beautiful park and its inhabitants all day, never missing a moment.

The younger tree, to its left, casts its eyes over to him, 'It's peaceful today,' he sighs contently.

'Yes, now the incessant drilling has stopped. I miss the simple times when we were surrounded by greenery beyond the park. All this concrete change feels wrong to me!'

The younger tree exhales deeply, 'I know, but at least they've protected us, and we can still hear the normal sounds of the park: the children laughing, adults chatting, dogs barking, nature going about its business. Not that much has changed.'

The elder tree remained steadfast in his opinion, verging on obstinate, 'it's all changed! Look to our right: they're building. Look to our left: they're building. I miss the simple times,' he stretches again, 'at least we have each other. At least that never changes.'

'But nothing really has changed. At the core of it all, we still have community.'

The trees look between them. The words have been cautiously whispered by the cast iron streetlamp, a long time unlit and un-utilised and she smiles, 'yes, it's all different and may look strange and unusual. But think of what we still see today. What we've seen every single day over the last hundred or so years. People. People make this park. The people are still here and, hopefully, will be for a long time to come. Yes, we're old. Yes, I'm neglected and go unnoticed, but we are still surrounded by people. By a community who enjoy this open space. We've been protected and remain for a reason: we are an important part of the park's history and we've seen it all. We still do. Every single day. And I stand by that.'

As if sensing this is their moment to help the elder tree, a child runs around his trunk. Laughing and hugging the tree's trunk. He exhales and smiles. In that moment, he remembers all the generations he has witnessed in this park, all the celebrations! The purchase and building of the fountain by Mr Harper; the birthday fetes in his honour; the stags, Earl and Harper and their mysterious disappearance; the Titanic commemoration; the Jubilee celebrations complete with bowling for chickens! He laughs at himself as he remembers that. Humans can be strange sometimes. However, despite their strangeness, he can't help but appreciate them. He then remembers the more recent times: the Park runs, the children who play in the park, the parents who chat over coffee, the owners walking their dogs, the walkers and the cyclists enjoying the park.

Maybe the streetlamp is right. Maybe, at its heart, the park re-mains the same: a place for peace, a place for play, a place for people and that will never really change. The heart of the park remains despite the seemingly never-ending urbanisation around them.

'You know what?'

The tree and lamp echo, in unison, 'What?'

'I think you're right. The heart remains the same.'

With that, the elder tree nestles down for another nap, content with the heart of what is around him. Peace. Play. People. And above all, community.

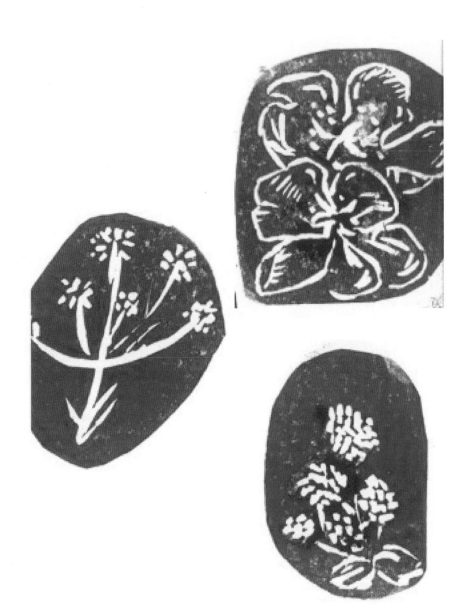

Little Things

Nicki Herring

When did I stop seeing little things?
The things an infant sees, sat ground-bound,
dandling fingers in the dust.

Was it when they said, 'Pay attention!'
to something an adult deemed more important
than mosquito larvae twig-stirred in a rusty tin?

Don't make him 'Hurry up', 'Walk quicker', 'Do big giant steps',
'Watch where you step' until he forgets where he is.

He'll learn your big important things.
Of course he will.

I see the breadcrumbs on the worktop
and dust on the skirting board.
Scum on the tap.
I deadhead the dahlias not seeing beauty in decay;
as lovely as the wrinkles on her older face.
I notice all the little things
I have not done,
still need to do.

Please stop.

Smell the bread and look to see
the jewels in the flowers in the dew.
It is alright to forget. Go back and look again.

We don't grow up or even old.

We think we do.
Children think they will.

Why have I distanced myself from the little things?
The dust. The rain drooped heads of cow parsley with
a thousand daisies held in every bud.

I have learnt to hold one hundred worries behind my eyes.

I no longer wrap my arms around a tree
and climb it, unconcerned about the fall.
It is late now, to be climbing for the view.

Too late to stretch lithe and tender limbs.

Is a tree a weed,
or a seed
grown far too tall?

Be quiet.

Listen.

What can you see up there? I want to know.

Don't be afraid that mud will turn to dirt on dusty feet.
Take off your shoes. Your sandals.
Feel the lively grass bending beneath your foot
that rises to a whisper on your sole.

Forget to keep off the grass.
We are all fellows of the earth.

Don't put your shoes on.

Run slower.
Have no great goal.
.
Stain your shirt and mouth and fingers with blackberries
eaten from the hedge.

Don't make him 'Hurry up', 'Walk quicker', 'Do big giant steps',
'Watch where you're going' until he forgets where he is.

Indulge in little things.

Look at the cow parsley.

Stop.

Stand.

Stare.

Neutral

Hope Jepson

Oxygen, Breathe

1... 2... 3... 4... in

There's a feeling you get,
             when scuba diving
weightless,

you are neither floating or sinking.

It's an other-worldly feeling,
             to be surrounded by the vast open
cobalt.

intense pressure frees
            – rather than constricts.

The only sound – the husk of the regulator.

1... 2... 3... 4... hold

Large lanterns strung to wicker baskets,
                    float on by
weightless,

drifting with the wind.

The chill blows away,
            The cobwebs gathering in my lungs.

The only sound – the roar of the burner.

1...2...3...4... out

Pace softly through the park,
                    It's autumn.

Flame reds, sunset oranges – yellows and burnt umbers file

                        one
                                    by
                                        one

down from the treetops.

The heartbeat my feet snuffles for smells.

The wind in the trees reminds me of my roaring breath in

the regulator,

The husk of the burner.

When all falls quiet,

            the only sound that remains constant, the crunch

of the leaves

                            and the patter of paws at
                            my feet.

Wish Granted!

Thierry Maillard

Little Roméo was the happiest boy alive today. So happy that he didn't mind running barefoot in the boiling sand, very clean but still very hot, all the way from where Julie had brought him to his mum. The Pokémon towels, the blue and white parasol, the football... everything was ready as if by magic, though he ran straight past her aiming for the sea instead.

"Roméo!"

He immediately stopped, frowned, and walked back slowly towards her. He grouched and even kicked an already half-destroyed sandcastle on his way. Meanwhile, his babysitter waved goodbye followed by a hand gesture meaning "See you tonight".

"The suncream's disgusting," he sat down with a huff, "how comes dad doesn't have to put some on?"

"Your dad's an idiot..."

He turned his head and stared at her, the frown on his face and his green amethyst eyes below showed her how he felt about that.

]"... sometimes."

As soon as she had finished smearing the dreaded suncream on him, he ran over, throwing a "can I go now?" at his mum. The answer seemed optional anyway. Little Roméo enjoyed the sea, much more than the hunting hikes his dad sometimes took him to.

She observed them for a while: Cédric was throwing Little Roméo in the water, and he was coming back to him for more.

She laid down, observing the sky, and tanning under the French sun.

Not a cloud on the horizon, or so she thought.

* * * * *

The merchant road was busier than ever. A plethora of languages had invaded the streets. How could it not be? Mimizan was a perfect holiday resort in the south-west of France. Sea, sun, many activities for everyone. In the middle of August, you'd be lucky if you could find space in a two-meter radius. In winter though, it was another story.

No sandwich, no croque-monsieur for lunch today. His parents had a surprise.

The blonde boy climbed the last step and realised he was entering a Moroccan restaurant. He looked back at his parents; his belly was rumbling like he last ate about a week ago. Why were adults so slow at going to places?

"Salam alaikum," the restaurant owner said opening the door.

Little Roméo was immediately overwhelmed by the colourfully patterned mirrors spread across the restaurant. Looking at the first one, he noticed his eyes were shinier than ever. It happens when it is very sunny. Unknown people, women mostly, sometimes stopped him in the street to comment on them.

"I'm cute!" he nodded to himself with pride.

His parents sat down at a table at the back. Little Roméo walked between oriental brass lanterns to reach the massive window behind them. Each lantern was adorned with white and dark blue eyes which seemed to follow every one of his movements. He was already under the funny impression he was being observed – he'd felt it earlier too at the beach. He was probably wrong.

 From that window, nearly as wide as a van, he had the best view of the merchant street: children devouring crepes or ice-creams, holidaymakers trying on various types of multicoloured sunglasses, teenagers browsing naughty postcards, not the ones you'd send to your mother.

A familiar face was walking down the street with a crepe in one hand and a boy on the other.

"Julie's there," he exclaimed, "she's with her boyfriend!"

The parents could not hear as they were disagreeing about whether they should order Bordeaux or Porto.

He kept pointing at all the people going up towards the beach. What would actually happen if too many people arrived on the beach at the same time? Would some be refused entry? Would they have to lay down on the road? It would take an awful lot of people for it to happen though; the fine sand beach was known as the Pearl of the Silver Coast and could probably host the whole regional population.

He felt like drawing the scene and adding it to the multiple drawings inundating his bedroom wall. Note for later, always carry a notepad and a pencil. Browsing the street up and down, he suddenly froze.

A bearded man.

He was looking straight at him.

I've been discovered!

The sound of broken glass deafened him. At the table, the parents, who were still debating the wine, did not hear a sound.

Little Roméo wondered if he was imagining this stranger staring at him. Hard to tell, but if he was, that's what it would look like.

"Jus d'orange ou jus de pomme?" his mum asked.

His heartbeats had never drummed that hard, even when he participated in the cross-country event in town three months ago. A warm arm enveloped him.

"What's the matter, ma puce?"

"Nothing, mum." His belly rumbled again. He looked at the street again.

Nothing.

Reassured, he eyed the smooth semolina and the delicious pieces of chicken which were waiting for him. He did not resist. His dad finished the last drops of Bordeaux.

* * * * * *

Cédric sounded the horn again.

"Mary!" Cédric shouted.

Little Roméo wouldn't let his mother go. Something was going to happen, he knew it.

He could hear the glass-breaking sound again and again in his mind.

"Roméo, we'll come back after the beach party. Julie is here with you."

"We'll have a game of boules now if you want," the baby-sitter exclaimed in an over-the-top happy voice.

"Your father won't be happy if we're late, you know that.

Little Roméo let his mother go. Julie already had the boules bag in one hand and led him toward the back garden with the other one.

"Who's the man with the blonde hair and the sunglasses in your drawing?" she asked, dropping the jack a few meters away.

"Dunno. Someone I saw today," he answered, annoyed it had been discovered. He knelt and threw his metallic boule near to the jack. "Shall we play War?" he asked with a puppy-like look. "Please…."

She frowned. "Do you even have cards?"

"Papa's got a silver box of poker cards and chips in 'the room' he uses with his friends."

The idea of going through the house to grab a pack of cards was about as appealing as running a hundred metres in heels. The boy still pulled a face.

"Promise to go to bed on time?"

He nodded.

She went to the kitchen, opened the oak cupboard and grabbed a key from an old rusty tea box hidden there.

"Stay there, prepare the table," she instructed him.

He complied and took the plates and empty glasses to the sink.

She walked away hesitantly. How she hated that room. The idea of entering it alone gave her the creeps, but Little Roméo was not allowed to accompany her in there. As soon as she opened the door, a draught travelled around her neck. The window was wide open. She closed it faster than she would dial her boyfriend's number. She walked on some broken glass. Great, another thing to clean.

She browsed the room. The room was plain, so were the walls: no wallpaper, no ornament of any sort, well if you exclude the rifle stack hung on the wall. Five of them in total. The only two pieces of furniture in the room were a small wooden cupboard where she would find the Poker set and a creepy antique wardrobe.

A creaking noise

She stared at the wardrobe but was not going to check. She opened the cupboard and grabbed the whole poker game before closing the door and locking it.

She never noticed the white shadow where one of the rifles used to be.

* * * * * *

"King of spades. I win," she exclaimed with a great smile.

"Not fair! You always win! "I wish I could know your cards."

"You need to find a wishing well then," she said.

"That doesn't even exist," he said.

"You know, there are over two hundred healing fountains in the Landes region. They say each one can heal a particular illness. Some heal verrucae, others skin diseases…"

Little Roméo pulled a face but let her talk.

"What many people don't know is that the La Fontaine St Jean in Rion -des-Landes is also a wishing well."

"Really?"

"Can you keep a secret?"

He nodded several times. Julie smiled. For once they could talk about something she enjoyed. Opening her bag and wallet in that order, she took out a photograph.

"This is Germain."

"I know. I've seen him several times. What about him?"

"I've had a crush on him since my first year in secondary school. He never talked to me or even looked at me. OK, I did not have much fashion sense back then and the competition was fierce: nearly every girl at school wanted him. The rumour around him was that no girl could keep him for more than a month."

"Did you ask him out?"

"That's the whole point: I didn't." she said. "A year ago, as soon as I got my driving licence, I drove to Rion-des-Landes and made my wish." She showed two fingers: "that's how many days it took my wish to come true."

"Just like that?" he asked.

"Just like that," she confirmed. "I have no clue how he got my number. All my friends swore they never gave it to him. On that day, he took me for a walk on the beach and we've been together since."

"Then can I wish to be rich?"

"The wish needs to come deep from your heart, and you also need to have faith."

"Can I make a wish to get more wishes?"

"Nope. The myth around the fountain is that you can only make one wish in your life."

She took out another photo of the fountain. This time a small hole on the ground was covered by a slate-tiled roof, surrounded by a red rounded brick wall smaller than him. Roméo couldn't hide his disappointment.

"It's not about what it looks like, but what it can do which matters." She looked at the clock, "time to go to bed."

"Last thing, how did you know your wish was going to happen?"

"Well, just after I made my wish, the unpleasant sound of broken glass echoed in my head. It happened a few times before it came true. Bedtime."

* * * * *

The baby-sitter heard a car parking outside.

"Half past twelve, 50 euros."

She was glad to leave as she was sure to have heard more noise from the 'forbidden room'. She never put the pack of cards back in the box where she found it and instead left it on the table next to the drawing of the strange man that she wanted to talk to his mum about.

She drew the kitchen curtains: it wasn't Romeo's father driving. It wasn't even his car. Aline, Cedric's sister, and her husband opened the front doors of the chrome Renault 21.

"Oh oh!"

The left passenger's side door opened. It took her a few long seconds to recognise Roméo's father. He came out, staggered on his feet and after a few steps fell down with a muffled sound.

"Jésus! Marc, help my brother," she said.

Her husband walked around the front of the car.

"Forgotten how to walk?" he giggled.

"Marc, don't!" Marie snapped. She noticed the baby-sitter was watching. She gave a look at Aline and walked towards their old farm house, searching her handbag.

Julie opened the door, took the money and put her hand on the mother's shoulder. Marie made a side movement with her head and the baby-sitter walked away.

Marc attempted to lift the body up, without success.

"You put weight on."

Thunder broke on the horizon. After the third attempt, he managed to lift his brother-in-law up easily. Too easily maybe... The inebriated man stood up filled with a newfound energy, his eyes staring with anger or confusion. Who knows. Aline saw her brother make an indistinct movement: her husband screamed and fell down. Blood dripped heavily from his hands.

"Are you crazy?" she screamed.

He smiled. He stumbled and managed to kick the side of the car violently.

"Stop it!" she shouted with her mobile phone in her right hand. "I'll call the police!"

"Call them. I'll shoot them all" he shouted even louder. He smirked at her and kicked her car a few more times.

"That's it!"

She dialled on her mobile phone. He walked towards her with a speed that she never expected, holding a clenched fist in the air.

"Don't you dare! I'm your sister."

Silence and darkness ensued. She couldn't feel it, but a light rain had started to fall.

* * * * *

"Eric, calme-toi !" Marie begged, rubbing her cheek better. Sitting on the floor, she surveyed the kitchen which was closer to a war scene than ever. Her mobile phone wasn't in sight. Was it buried under the remnants of the table or under the broken plates? Hopefully the elderly neighbours would have heard the noise and made the phone call she should have made years ago. Hopefully Little Romeo would not have heard anything.

He held a teacup in his hand. It was half of the pair they received for their first-year anniversary. He looked at her.

"Cédric, you're gonna wake-"

"Je m'en fous !" he screeched, throwing the cup which only missed Marie by a few centimetres.

"It's over!" she sobbed.

"Yeah, you're right about that." He stormed into the corridor, bumping into the walls. She opened her eyes wide when she heard her husband kick a door once, twice and more until a crashing noise reached her... Suddenly her blood froze: Roméo!

He left his room and rushed into her arms while her father was inside the 'forbidden room'. He sobbed uncontrollably. She stood up with him and walked towards the door.

"Where do you think you're going?" an unrecognisable voice coming from her husband said.

"Cédric, put that down!"

She knew her husband was a good shot, he always said it ran in the family and always would, even with an ancient model like a French Robust shotgun.

"You have ruined this evening like you've ruined my entire life!" he shouted.

"Cédric, it's not-"

"Stop calling my name!"

He aimed his barrel towards her. Without hesitation, she pushed a frozen Little Roméo behind her.

* * * * *

A broken window.

The deafening sound of a shotgun.

Screams.

* * * * *

Nobody moved, nobody breathed for what seemed like hours.

A mixed sound of broken glass and a water fountain that only the people who were conscious could hear broke the silence. Little Roméo remembered it.

The front door opened. Slowly, Mary turned her head. A bearded stranger she had never met entered. He put the rifle he was holding on the floor next to Little Roméo's drawing. She was speechless when she noticed the resemblance between the drawing and the man's face.

"You're safe now."

He knelt before her. Tears were flowing down his green-amethyst eyes. Tears of pain, tears of joy.

The man hugged both the woman and her child.

"Oh, I've missed you so much, mum!"

* * * * *

Powerful rotating blue lights in the street reached the kitchen. Big Romeo stood up and noticed the police car outside.

Little Romeo found the courage to look at the stranger. He smiled; he had been right; he had really been staring at him earlier at the restaurant.

Big Roméo's clothes, even his body, were gradually losing their opacity.

As he was disappearing, he could not take his eyes off them. Before he evaporated totally, he smiled at them one last time and whispered: "Wish granted".

The Old Tree

Old with time
Acre of trees
Home to birds
Squirrels running up branches
Dogs and owners walking each other
Children flying kites
up up in the air
Children pick up leaves
Go home make pictures

Toni Minns

'Hello Autumn'

Claire Oliver

Two friends meet like odd socks, to walk a familiar rickety path, never mind these blistering puddles that remind us of when we drank Club orange in the summer heat. This ice will melt, as will this thick grey atmosphere, our voices frozen in time like a Victorian nursery rhyme. Our friendship is sprinkled with rainbow glitter, shoulder to shoulder we walk a little less severely. Our feet strumming through life's muddles, rain spray soaking our tan nylons, my polka dot brolly, twirling rhythmically like our biological clocks, this wet road we take now running downhill towards the end of bright days. Wet mornings, dark afternoons, our breath lingering in the icy air, no bird song or chatter of expectant mothers, their older tots screaming to be pushed, their tiny plump legs soaring through the air, with red shiny shoes. The look of content acceptance from our wrinkled faces, our walk with nature will continue to be carried in the whispers of the fallen leaves.

In Autumn the sun falls at our feet, it kisses us goodbye through nature and leaves us for Winter, soaking us in gold, drenched in copper and folds us in bronze and ochre.

'I am'

Claire Oliver

I am a piece, a drop, a speck a fragment this world does not feel.

I am a dancer, a dreamer, a listener, a writer, a page the world will not read.

I am a voyager, an explorer, a passion, an anarchist, a thought the world will not hear.

I am in love, an escapist, a warrior, a stranger, an animal the world does not fear.

I am home, I am renewed, a joy, a wish come through, a familiarity the world does not see.

I am her, her mother, her existence, I am forever her, a world will not miss me.

I am fallen, a lost soul, a shadow, a memory, a ghost, a world does not believe in.

I am him, his mother, his smile, his burning light, an energy the world did not conceive.

I am now found, complete, a mother, a wife, a beat as steady as a poetic line, this world is now and will, forever be mine.

Ode to Tony

Claire Oliver

As a young boy I set my toy boat afloat in the Victorian fountain at the park,

I daydreamed of when I'd be a grown man, and captain of the Cutty Stark.

Now I stand upon the sands, my footprints of a man,

My dreams of voyage and adventure did not go to plan.

I stand and gaze at the blue horizon, the crew I will no longer greet, the morning tide came in so fast, the cold waves lapped at my feet.

The 'Man of War' with masts so high her canvas blowing free, off to conquer foreign lands while her bow cuts through the sea.

Oh, to be upon her deck and count the stars above, the freedom of the ocean waves would be my only love.

To see the dolphins guide us home, the gulls above us follow, the pride I'd feel for our King & Queen would make it hard for me to swallow,

...and now I wake from my daydream to find her gone, what tales I'll have to tell.

The ocean is my only love, my great giant wishing well.

Midnight Garden

Sita Turner

When the stars shine as mineral dust in a Nordic sky
She awakens
Silently heralded by three or four petals that
Unfurl from their downy beds, their contoured veins
Directing nectar hungry bees towards a
Pollen dusted core.

Under covert sapphire she whispers secrets
To the visitors that busy themselves
Within architectural cities under her
Furrowed earth, while fleshy roots
Spread succulent arms to charter new
Courses through the soil.

She has a distinctive scent of vanilla, honey and almonds
Magnified by velvet night
Heightened by moonlight whose beams
Rain down upon her clustered heads.

The midnight microclimate suits her tenderness well:
By day, the sun directs a performance
Starring flowers and plants who bathe in humidity
Allowing insects to visit them with careless frequency.
Too much drama
She smiles as a cat stretches himself out lithely
At the shadowy borders.
Jasmine and Primrose nod their heads in solidarity.

As the scorching seductress rises in the blanched sky,
She extinguishes the firefly candles,
Moisturises the clavicle trees with dew

And closes her weary eyes.

Soon Asteria will tap her shoulder
And the midnight garden will awaken
Once again.

Acknowledgements

We would like to extend our thanks to Ashford Borough Council and the Victoria Park project for encouraging this collaboration from its infancy. Special thanks go to Victoria Fannon who ensured everything was in place for us and championed the idea from the start.

We would also like to thank everyone at Harper's Café for their friendliness and for keeping our brains fuelled with pastries and coffee!

Printed in Great Britain
by Amazon

35783532R00023